WELCOME TO
PASSPORT TO READING
A beginning reader's ticket to a brand-new world!

Every book in this program is designed to build read-along and read-alone skills, level by level, through engaging and enriching stories. As the reader turns each page, he or she will become more confident with new vocabulary, sight words, and comprehension.

These PASSPORT TO READING levels will help you choose the perfect book for every reader.

READING TOGETHER
Read short words in simple sentence structures together to begin a reader's journey.

READING OUT LOUD
Encourage developing readers to sound out words in more complex stories with simple vocabulary.

READING INDEPENDENTLY
Newly independent readers gain confidence reading more complex sentences with higher word counts.

READY TO READ MORE
Readers prepare for chapter books with fewer illustrations and longer paragraphs.

This book features sight words from the educator-supported Dolch Sight Words List. This encourages the reader to recognize commonly used vocabulary words, increasing reading speed and fluency.

For more information, please visit passporttoreadingbooks.com.

Enjoy the journey!

Little, Brown and Company

Hachette Book Group
1290 Avenue of the Americas, New York, NY 10104
Visit our website at lb-kids.com

Little, Brown and Company is a division of Hachette Book Group, Inc.
The Little, Brown name and logo are trademarks of Hachette Book Group, Inc.

The publisher is not responsible for websites (or their content) that are not owned
by the publisher.

First Edition: July 2014

Library of Congress Cataloging-in-Publication Data

Gall, Chris, author, illustrator.
Dinotrux go to school / Chris Gall. — First edition.
pages cm. — (Passport to reading. Level 1)
Summary: Prehistoric part-dinosaur part-truck machines help each other
get ready for their first day of school.
ISBN 978-0-316-40062-6 (hardcover) — ISBN 978-0-316-40061-9 (pbk.)
[1. Imaginary creatures—Fiction. 2. Trucks—Fiction.
3. First day of school—Fiction.] I. Title.
PZ7.G1352Dk 2014
[E]—dc23
2013028457

10 9 8 7 6 5 4 3 2

SC

Printed in China

DINOTRUX
GO TO SCHOOL

CHRIS GALL

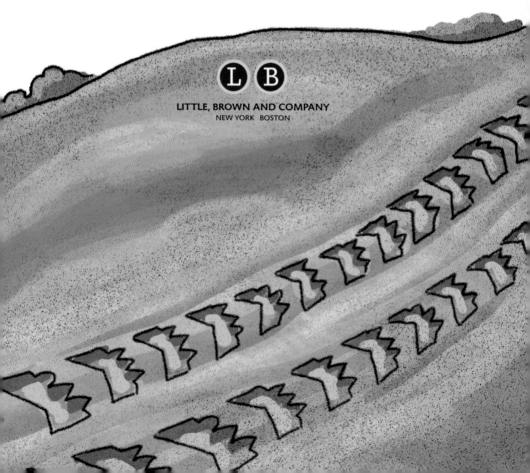

L B

LITTLE, BROWN AND COMPANY
NEW YORK   BOSTON

GUIDE TO THE DINOTRUX

CEMENTOSAURUS
seh • men • toh • SOR • us

CRANEOSAURUS
cray • nee • oh • SOR • us

DELIVERADON
deh • LI • ver • uh • don

DIGASAURUS
dig • uh • SOR • us

DUMPLODUCUS
dump • luh • DUH • kus

DOZERATOPS
doh • ZAIR • uh • tops

GARBAGEADON
gar • BAJ • uh • don

ROLLODON
ROHL • oh • don

SEMISAURUS
sem • ee • SOR • us

SEPTISAURUS
sep • ti • SOR • us

TANKERSAURUS
tank • er • SOR • us

TOWADON
TOH • uh • don

TYRANNOSAURUS TRUX
ty • RAN • oh • sor • us TRUKS

The Dinotrux woke up.

The sun was shining.

But summer was over.

It was the first day of school.

"I do not want to go to school,"
said Dumploducus.

"We will go together," said Craneosaurus.

Craneosaurus lifted Dumploducus
out of bed.

The Semisaurs rumbled by.

"Do not be late! Do not be late!" they said.

Dozeratops pushed boulders out of the way.
"I will clear our path to school," he said.

"This year, we will have much to learn,"
Craneosaurus said. "We will need books."
He loaded Dumploducus with books.

The books were very heavy.

Dumploducus could barely move his tires.

"I will tow you to school," said Towadon.

Rollodon rolled up.

"We will need supplies," he said.

He rolled on top of some logs.

He rolled and rolled until the logs were flat.

"Now we have lots of paper!" he cried.

Garbageadon heard his stomach growl.
"What if there is not enough food
for lunch?" he said.
"What if I run out of gas?"

"I will bring extra food for you,"
said Deliveradon.

Tyrannosaurus Trux was worried.

"I hope our teacher is not a giant, smelly caveman," he said.

Digasaurus drew a picture in the dirt.

"Like this?" said Digasaurus.

Tyrannosaurus Trux laughed.

"Yes! If he is scary, I will show him my teeth!"

Cementosaurus was upset.

"Is there a bathroom at school?"
he asked.

"Of course," said Garbageadon.

"I have to go all the time,"
said Cementosaurus.

"I know. Just raise your hand like
this," said Garbageadon.

"Will we have juice?" cried Septisaurus.

"I will fill my tank with juice
for everyone," said Tankersaurus.

"Thank you, Tankersaurus.

I need lots of juice!" Septisaurus said.

He let out a sigh of relief.

The Dinotrux arrived at school.

Garbageadon found the garbage can.

Dozeratops moved the desks to make room.

Digasaurus drew on the chalkboard.

Tyrannosaurus Trux found a new box of pencils.

Then he chomped the box in half.

"Now there will be enough for all of us!"
he roared.

The teacher came into the classroom.

He was a giant, smelly caveman.

He was carrying three big clubs.

The Dinotrux trembled in fear.

"It is not possible!" shouted Digasaurus.

"He looks just like my drawing!"

The bell rang.

The teacher started to juggle.

The Dinotrux laughed.

School was not so scary after all.

They were together with friends.

And it would soon be time for recess!